To Blake,
Barbara
Davoll

FOUL PLAY
AT MOLER PARK

WRITTEN BY

Barbara Davoll

Pictures by Dennis Hockerman

MOODY PRESS
CHICAGO

D1319284

To our granddaughter,
Bethany Lynaé Davoll,
daughter of Jeffrey J. and Deanne E. Davoll,
for bringing us great joy
as our first grandchild

Moody Press, a ministry of the Moody Bible Institute,
is designed for education, evangelization, and edifi-
cation. If we may assist you in knowing more about
Christ and the Christian life, please write us without
obligation: Moody Press, c/o MLM, Chicago, IL 60610.
Printed in MEXICO.

ISBN: 0-8024-2703-0

Children love the stories of Barbara Davoll, known for her award-winning, best-selling Christopher Churchmouse Classics and now for the Molehole Mystery series. Barbara writes these zany new adventures in Schroon Lake, New York where she and her husband, Roy, minister at home and abroad with Word of Life International in their Missions Department. Barb manages to stay busy as a wife, mother, grandmother, author, drama teacher, church musician, and homemaker for her husband and Josh, the family Schnauzer.

Illustrator Dennis Hockerman has concentrated on art for children's trade books and textbooks, magazines, greeting cards, and games. He lives with his wife and three children in Mequon, Wisconsin, a suburb of Milwaukee. Mr. Hockerman probably spent more time "underground" than above while developing the characters and creating the etchings for the Molehole Mysteries. Periodically, he would poke his head into his "upstairs connection" to join his family and share with them the adventures of his friends in Molesbury R.F.D.

Contents

1. WHODUNIT? 9

2. THE DISAPPEARING ACT 19

3. THE BROKEN BENCH 27

4. ALBY'S PLAN 35

5. TO CATCH A SHREW 43

6. THE MISSING NOTEBOOK 51

7. TRIP TO SHREWSVILLE 59

8. THE MOLERS' STRATEGY 67

9. ALMOST OUT 73

10. THE ALL-STAR 81

    THROUGH THE SPYGLASS 91

WHODUNIT?

Dusty and Musty Mole, junior agents, and several of the Molehole Mystery Club gang sat in the stands of Shrew Park with their eyes glued to the ballfield. It was the last inning of an exciting baseball game between their team, the Mighty Molers, and the Scramblin' Shrews.

The Molers held their breath as the Shrews came to bat in the bottom of the ninth. Although the Molers were leading 1-0, they were facing the top of the Shrew's batting order in this last inning.

Two runs by the Shrews would put the Molers out of the underground play-off. That had never happened before, but the little moles knew it was a possibility this time. The Shrews had the advantage of playing on their home field today. The way the score stood after this inning would determine the winner.

The first Shrew up to bat grounded out, and the Molers roared their approval. Only two more outs and they were in the play-off.

The Molers' pitcher, Snarkey Mole, looked at the catcher, tugged on his cap, and shook off a sign. He got the second sign, went into the stretch, and threw the ball. The Shrew batter hit a ground ball to the shortstop that went right through his legs. He missed the easy play, and the Shrew runner went to first base on an error.

"Oh no," groaned Dusty, as he jumped to his feet. "We should have had that one!"

His sister, Musty, clutched her friend Penney's paw. "That's the tying run on base," she squealed.

Penney sat with her fingers crossed and her small mole eyes squeezed shut. She didn't know much about baseball, but she surely wanted the moles to win. "I can't bear to look," she said breathlessly, her paws over her eyes.

The next hit was a blooper to right field that dropped in for a single. This advanced the Shrew runner to third base—only a short distance from home plate and the tying run.

"Come on, Snarkey!" yelled Dusty to Snarkey, who was also an important member of the Molehole Mystery Club. "Give 'em your fast ball!"

Otis, another Molehole Mystery Club member, stood on the sidelines as the Molers' batboy, anxiously watching his pal Snarkey. "You can do it, Snarkey! Settle down and pitch your funny curve ball!"

Just then a gasp went up from the section of seats where the Moler fans sat. The reason for the gasp was that the next batter was Sammy Shrew, Jr., son of the feared Sammy Shrew. He was the ace of the Shrew team and a dirty player, well-known for his tricks and cheating.

Sammy, Jr., stepped to the plate and faced Snarkey with a snarl. "Come on, you mushy mole. Give me one I can put outa here," he growled.

Penney uncovered her eyes just in time to see Sammy's father enter the stadium on the other side of the field and join the Shrew fans. Grabbing Morty, who sat next to her, she squealed, "Look, Morty! It's that awful Sammy Shrew!"

"I know, Penney," said Morty, trying not to lose patience with the little girl mole who knew so little about the game. "He's up to bat and will try to hit the ball."

"No, Morty! I *know* he's up to bat. I mean Sammy's father, Sammy Shrew, Sr., is here. He just walked in over on their side."

"So he did," mumbled Morty, squinting across the field. "I can't believe he'd come out in the open. The police have had him on their Most Wanted List since he escaped from jail."

"Shows you how important this game is to the Shrews. They don't want to enter the play-off against us," observed Dusty. "Here comes the pitch, girls," he snapped to Musty and Penney. They were chattering about Sammy Shrew and paying little attention to the game. It always disgusted the boys that the girl moles seemed to come to games only to visit with each other.

Snarkey delivered a scorching fastball to the feared Shrew slugger. Sammy connected with a fierce crack of the bat. The ball streaked up the middle toward center field, and the Moler shortstop, who had made the previous error, snagged it on the tip of his glove. He flipped it to second base.

The Molers' second baseman turned to throw to first, but he was upended by the Shrew coming to second base. The ball, thrown wildly into the dirt, was scooped up by the Molers' first baseman. Sammy was beaten by a half step to complete the double play.

That won the game for the Molers, sending them into the championship play-off. The moles went wild, screaming and cheering as Snarkey was carried off the field by his happy teammates.

"Let's get down there," yelled Dusty as he jumped the stadium seats to get to his friends for the time of celebration.

Morty Mole held out his paw to the girl moles to help them down over the seats toward the field.

Just then a ball thrown from somewhere hit Snarkey full force, and he crumpled over in pain. He was caught by his teammates who were holding him above their heads. A gasp went up from the mole fans who saw it happen.

"Hey! Who threw that?" yelled Otis, as they anxiously lowered their pitcher to the ground. Dusty was already on his way, jumping over the wall to reach the crowd standing around his injured friend. Musty and Penney stood paralyzed, looking at the now silent crowd.

Who had thrown that ball? The joy the little moles felt had quickly turned to fear.

THE DISAPPEARING ACT

Musty and Penney anxiously followed Dusty and Morty to the field and joined the silent group of animals around Snarkey. For a couple of minutes, the Molers' pitcher did not move. Then he slowly opened his narrow eyes and blinked at the faces staring down at him.

"Make way," commanded the worried voice of the Molers' coach. "Give him air!" Roughly he shoved the animals aside and knelt over his prize pitcher.

"Where did the ball hit you, Snarkey?" asked the coach as Snarkey began to come to.

"Got him on the side of the head," answered Otis. He was kneeling on the other side, fanning his friend with his cap.

"Did anyone see where it came from?" asked the coach, looking up.

"No sir! Just whizzed past me from over there," answered a mole, pointing toward the Shrew dugout.

"Must have been one of the Shrew team," concluded another mole.

"We don't know for sure that it was a Shrew," warned Dusty, who was examining the ball. "This ball is just like the ones we use. There's no way to tell if it came from the Shrews or not."

By now Snarkey was sitting up in a daze, rubbing a large knot on the side of his head. The coach helped him lie down on the stretcher that had been brought over by some medics.

"Take him to the Molesbury Hospital," commanded the coach. "I want X-rays and a full report of his condition. I'll join you there as soon as I can." As Snarkey was carried from the field, the coach signaled Dusty to stay behind.

"Dusty, I want you and your Mystery Club gang to find out who threw that ball. Snarkey could have been killed. We can't have that going on."

"I'll get on it right away, Coach. Snarkey's one of our club members. You can be sure we'll do our best to solve this one."

Dusty was joined by the other Mystery Club members, and they walked slowly from the field, talking about the mysterious ball and Snarkey's injury.

"I'll be right back," said Dusty. "I want to see what they're saying in the locker-room. Wait here for me and keep your eyes open for anything that seems unusual."

When Dusty entered the locker-room, most of the moles were already in the showers. He found Otis counting balls and putting equipment away. The chubby mole looked up, scratching his head in a puzzled way.

"What's wrong, Otis?" asked Dusty.

"I'm missing three baseballs," replied Otis. "They were here when we started the game because I counted them. Now where do you suppose they went?" he mumbled, stooping to look under the benches.

"I'll help you look," volunteered Dusty. Together they searched the locker-room but found nothing.

"Let's look in the lockers while the guys are in the showers," suggested Dusty.

"We aren't allowed in each other's lockers. That's against the rules," growled Otis. He was tired and upset.

"How about these lockers over here?" called Dusty from across the room. He was pointing to a group of lockers along the opposite wall. "Are these lockers assigned to anyone?"

"Naw, they're extras. We never use them," muttered Otis, with his head down in the bag of balls, trying to recount them.

Dusty pulled open the first locker and found nothing but dirt. Then he pulled the second one open. "Otis!" he called with excitement. "Here they are!"

"Well, I'll be," exclaimed Otis. "How'd they get in there?" he wondered, coming over to see for himself. Scooping them up, he put them away in the ball bag. "If that doesn't beat all," he grumbled, shaking his head. "This job is no picnic anymore."

"What do you mean?" asked his friend.

"I mean, with Snarkey getting hurt and all. Now these balls—I mean, that's not serious—but who would do it—and why?"

"I don't know, but I mean to find out," answered the private eye, with a look on his face that meant business.

THE BROKEN BENCH

All the moles anxiously awaited word from the hospital as to Snarkey's condition. They were relieved to hear that he would be all right, although the doctor said he had a concussion. The alarming news was that he couldn't play ball for two weeks.

That information really depressed the moles. The play-off was in just three weeks. That meant their best pitcher would miss most of the play-off practice.

A couple of days later Dusty called a meeting of the Molehole Mystery Club to report his findings about Snarkey's injury. Just as the meeting was called to order, Snarkey walked into the clubhouse.

"Well, look who's here," said Dusty happily. Penney ran to get Snarkey a chair. The other members hovered around him excitedly, asking how he felt.

"Do you think you can play in the play-off game?" asked Millard Mole with concern.

"Sure hope so," responded Snarkey. "I can't practice much before that," he added glumly.

"Well, cheer up," said Morty, who was always optimistic. "I'm sure the other guys will do their best at pitching, and you don't need much practice anyway."

"You said it," said Otis enthusiastically. All the members cheered and clapped, trying to encourage their downcast friend.

"We're just giving our reports about your injury," said Dusty. "I'm afraid I don't have much to report myself. I couldn't find anyone who saw anything except your being carried off the field by your teammates."

"That's what the Shrews were counting on," growled Otis. "They knew they could get away with such a mean trick."

The others agreed. Then Otis spoke up again. "You know those balls we found in the locker, Dusty?"

Dusty nodded.

"Well, more strange things have been happening. It seems every day something happens to keep us from our practice."

"Like what?" quizzed Dusty.

"Well, like the day after Snarkey was injured. We were all ready to start practice and couldn't find the bats. I'd laid them down by home plate, and while I was getting out the catcher's equipment, the bats disappeared."

"Disappeared?" snarled Morty. "How could they disappear?"

"I don't know. I had my head down in the bag getting out the other stuff. Anybody could have taken them. Delayed our practice a half hour trying to find them.

"But that isn't all," he went on. "The next day when it was real hot, one of the guys took a big swig out of the water jug. It was full of mud," he said with disgust.

"Who is doing all this?" cried Musty.

"And why?" wondered Snarkey, who sat with his bandaged head in his hands, thinking.

"It must be the Shrews," observed Penney.

"They're trying to sabotage us and keep us from practice," muttered Snarkey. "They know that with me laid up, the other pitchers will need practice. If they can keep us from practice they can win the championship."

Suddenly Dusty's eyes lit up the way they usually did when he had a plan. "Otis, you need another batboy on the team, don't you?" asked the junior agent.

"Well, no, I can handle it all right," began Otis. "Who did you want—" As the chubby mole looked at Dusty he stopped his sentence in mid-air. "Oh!" he exclaimed, understanding. "You mean you."

Dusty laughed. "That's right! I think I'll become a batboy for the mole team. You and I can check this out together."

The next day Dusty showed up just as the moles were arriving for practice. He and Otis walked over to the coach, who was working on his stats notebook.

"Coach, Dusty is going to help me with the equipment and stuff since we've been having so much trouble. Is that OK?" asked Otis with a wink.

The coach quickly caught onto the reason Dusty wanted to hang around. "Sure," he agreed. "We can always use an extra hand around here."

Dusty helped Otis get out the equipment for practice, alert to anything out of the ordinary.

Everything seemed normal as the Molers took the field and began their practice game. The moles waiting their turn to bat filed out of the dugout and sat on the bench near home plate.

Suddenly, there was a loud *CRACK!* Dusty saw the whole row of moles who were sitting on the bench dumped to the ground. The bench had collapsed! With much scrambling they got to their feet, brushing themselves off and grumbling.

"What caused that?" yelled the coach as he came running to see what had happened.

"This bench just gave way," yelled Otis.

"Guess we're too heavy for it," quipped a mole who had been sitting there.

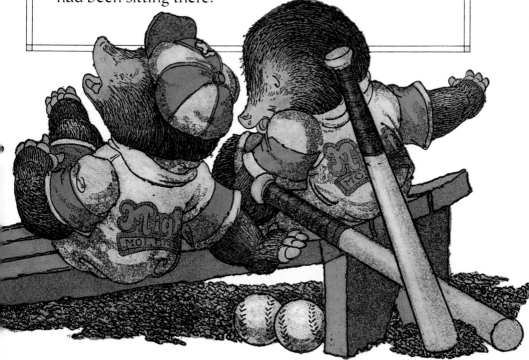

Dusty ran to the collapsed bench and began to examine it. "It wasn't too much weight that caused it to collapse," he said quietly, looking up. He was holding a broken piece of the bench in his paws. "This board has been sawed through so that it would break when you sat on it."

ALBY'S PLAN

An emergency meeting of the Mystery Club was called that evening. All the club members stood quietly talking in the clubhouse, waiting for Dusty to arrive. They realized how serious the situation had become.

Mortimer Mole stood talking with Otis and Snarkey. "Who knows what will happen next?" he remarked.

"Here comes Dusty now," called Penney, who'd been watching out the clubhouse window.

"Hi, gang," greeted their leader. "Have a seat so we can get started. Millard, read us the minutes from our last meeting."

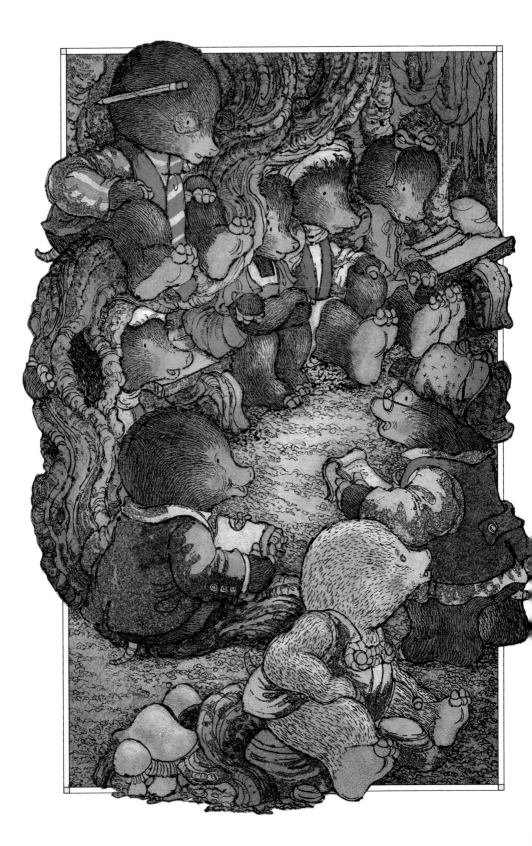

Millard read the minutes, which brought the members up-to-date on all that had taken place. When Millard finished, Dusty said he had a new development to report.

"Today I met an old friend who knows several shrews very well," he said. "He told me that Sammy Shrew's father has been bragging all over Shrewsville that he took care of Snarkey Mole. He claims Snarkey won't pitch in the championship. It seems he's wanted to get even with Snarkey for a long time since he helped crack Sammy Shrew's drug ring."[1]

"Dusty! That's wonderful! Now we know who did it," shrieked Musty happily.

"Certainly seems so," agreed Dusty, "but we have to prove it to bring him to justice. How to do that is another thing."

"Why don't we just try to catch him and make him admit it?" asked Penney.

"You don't catch Sammy Shrew that easily," replied Mortimer. "He's very sneaky."

"Catching him would be like catching the measles." Penney shuddered. "What would you do with him once you caught him?"

---

[1] Read about this in *Dusty Mole, Private Eye*.

"Make him talk and then pack him off to jail where he belongs," snapped Otis. "They have enough on him to send him to jail for years."

"Yeah, but they can't keep him in jail. He's too ornery. Keeps escaping," said Mort.

"We sure need to put him behind bars," agreed Dusty. "If we don't, he can pull anything, especially with Sammy, Jr., playing for the Shrews. What we need is a lure. Something to get him out in the open."

"Does Sammy and his gang still use that old hideout in the swamp?" asked Snarkey.

"I think so," answered the junior agent. "But you can't get near it. They have guards and lookouts all around it day and night."

"How about setting up a scrimmage game between the Shrews and the Molers before the play-offs?" asked Morty. "You know, sort of a mock championship challenge between Sammy, Jr., and Flash Mole, our best hitter. Sammy's father would come out for that, I bet."

"He'd probably try to harm Flash or something," observed Alby Mole. Alby was a small, white albino mole who had recently become a member of the Molehole Mystery Club. He was very quiet and hardly ever made suggestions, thinking he was too new to say much about detective work.

"Alby! You've got it!" yelled Dusty. He was always quick to encourage the members and make them think they had contributed something.

"I do?" asked Alby in a dazed tone.

"You sure do! He'd probably attempt to hurt Flash. If we could catch him at it, we'd nail him for sure," said Dusty with confidence. "Now let's figure out our plan."

Alby flushed with pleasure to think he could help in solving a difficult case like this one. The shy mole was still not used to having friends who listened to him.

"Otis, you have Coach Malley set up a challenge before the play-off," directed Dusty. Carefully the members devised a plan to catch Sammy Shrew, Sr.

They would disguise themselves as Shrew fans so they could sit among the Shrews. They were sure Sammy, Sr., would come to see his son challenge Flash. When Sammy's father made a wrong move, as they were sure he would, they would capture him and have the evidence needed to jail him.

"What can Penney and I do?" asked Musty. "We want to help, don't we, Penney?"

Penney nodded, bravely gulping back her fear. The stories of the notorious Sammy Shrew really frightened her.

"Otis, ask Coach Malley if Musty and Penney can join the Molers," instructed Dusty. "That way they'll be on hand to help if we need them."

Mortimer gave a hard look at Dusty. "They don't have any girls on the Molers," he said with a hint of his old prejudice against girls.

"No reason they can't," asserted Dusty. "I'm sure it will be fine with the coach and team. After all, Musty plays ball on the girls' team and throws a mean curve ball. Penney will learn quickly, I'm sure."

Musty's mole eyes widened at this unexpected praise from her brother. "Oh, wow! Let's go practice, Penney! We're going to join the Molers!"

TO CATCH A SHREW

The day of the challenge, Moler Park was packed with moles and shrews, all waiting excitedly to see Sammy, Jr., and Flash slug it out with their bats.

Everything went as Dusty expected and planned. Flash out-hit Sammy three to one. His father, Sammy Shrew, Sr., showed up near the end, disguised as a very old shrew. Morty, sitting next to Dusty, gave him a poke when he saw the bent-over figure enter the stands.

"There he is!" he whispered with excitement. "I'd know that conceited animal anywhere, no matter what disguise he's wearing."

"You said it!" agreed Dusty in a low tone. "Don't take your eyes off him. He's sure to pull something."

Just as the challenge was ending, Dusty saw Sammy, Sr., reach into the long coat he was wearing and bring out a large bottle. The moles, watching carefully, saw him pretend to take a drink from it. Then he drew back his paw to throw the bottle at Flash down on the playing field.

Instantly a signal flashed from Dusty, and the shrew was surrounded by Molehole Mystery Club members and the Molesbury police. Clapping handcuffs on him, they took him away to jail.

"Boy! Those police moved in quickly, didn't they?" remarked Morty to Dusty as they were leaving the stands.

"You bet! They were glad to get him. He's done so much harm since he escaped this last time," agreed the private eye.

"Let's just hope they can keep him in there. He's really sly and quick as a greased pig at getting out," quipped Morty.

Just then Otis yelled to Dusty from the field below. "Hey, Dusty! Come quick! We need you!"

Dusty excused himself from his friends and jumped down onto the field. As he raced into the locker-room, Otis said, "You aren't going to believe this, Dusty! While we were having the contest, our good uniforms were stolen!"

Dusty stared in disbelief at the mole team and their coach. Sure enough, the closet where the uniforms usually hung was empty. The broken lock was lying on the floor.

Coach Malley was angrily pacing the floor. "I just don't understand who is doing this," he growled, his

heavy jowls wiggling up and down as he walked.

"I can tell you who it isn't," observed Dusty.

The team and coach stared at him.

"It isn't Sammy Shrew, Sr.," he explained. "We just captured him, and the police are taking him to jail."

Ferdie Ferret, the Molers' second baseman, gasped. "What do you mean, jail?" he growled.

"We caught him trying to throw a bottle at Flash," explained Dusty further. "We're sure he's the one who threw the ball at Snarkey. The police just captured him and returned him to jail."

"That's great!" responded Ferdie, burying his head in his locker and fishing around for his clothes.

Dusty looked at him carefully. Something about Ferdie's tone of voice troubled him.

"Yeah, but that doesn't solve our problem about everything else that's happening around here," observed Otis.

Coach Malley looked blankly at Dusty and asked, "Where do we go from here?"

"I'm sorry, Coach Malley, I don't know," answered Dusty. "I thought if we jailed the shrew, all our troubles would be over. The only thing I know so far is that he is the one who tried to harm Snarkey. It looks as though someone else is trying to sabotage the team."

Just then Ferdie Ferret barged into the room. He had gone to the shower while Dusty continued talking with the coach and other team members. The ferret, wrapped in a towel, pulled his locker open with a bang and began to dress. He seemed in a hurry.

"What's your rush, Ferdie?" demanded Otis, a bit annoyed at the noise the ferret was making.

"Yeah! You sure got out of the shower fast," observed Snarkey.

"Where's the fire?" asked Dusty.

"I don't talk to *outsiders*," sniffed Ferdie, looking at Dusty in a suspicious way. Quickly he stuffed his things into a gym bag and left the locker-room with his nose in the air.

"What brought that on?" asked Dusty.

"Aw, pay no attention to him," explained Otis. "He's always in a snit. Acts like he's got a burr under his tail."

"Hmm," said Dusty. "How long has he been on the team?" he asked casually.

"He joined us this year," answered the coach. "He's on the second string and doing well. Ferrets are larger than moles, and sometimes clumsy. But he is overcoming that."

"He sure has a bad attitude," remarked Snarkey. "He's always edgy and nasty."

"Well, the poor kid has a bad home life," said Coach Malley. "We need to give him a chance. There's more to being on this team than being a good ball player. I hope we can help Ferdie make something of himself and have a better attitude in life."

The team headed for the showers, and Dusty walked thoughtfully across the field to join his friends. Maybe he had a lead. *Could Ferdie be the culprit causing all the trouble? If so, why?*

THE MISSING NOTEBOOK

The next day the Molers' practice was exciting. Coach Malley divided them into two teams, with the girl moles on different sides.

Musty's team was in the field, and the bases were loaded. Flash Mole was up to bat and hit a long ball, which looked as if it could be a home run.

Musty, playing in right field, looked up squinting at the ball, which was far above her reach. With a flying leap she caught it in mid-air for the third out. Falling into the dust she held onto it as her team won the practice game.

Triumphantly the little girl mole started to pick herself up. Just then an animal flew past her and pushed her face down into the dirt again.

"Hey! What do you think you're doing?" yelled the outraged Musty. Jumping up, she raced after the animal that had shoved her so roughly. She was fast, but not fast enough to catch the rude animal.

Suddenly a mole jumped out from the bleachers and grabbed the animal Musty was chasing.

"Not so fast, Buster!" cried Dusty, scuffling with the animal.

Through clouds of dirt Musty saw that Dusty had hold of Ferdie Ferret. "He tried to—" she panted.

"I know," interrupted Dusty. "I was watching. Why did you shove Musty in the dirt?" he demanded of the ferret.

"I—didn't—mean to—" Ferdie gasped for air.

"You did too!" retorted Musty angrily.

"Yes, you did, Ferdie. I saw what you did to my sister, and I didn't like it one bit," spit Dusty.

The mole, who still had hold of the ferret's uniform, pulled him up close and, looking him in the eye, threatened him. "I'll be watching you from now on, Ferdie. See that you never pull a mean trick like that again."

With a little shake he loosed Ferdie, who shuffled away with a snarl. The rest of the team crowded around, wanting to know if Musty was all right.

"That was some catch, Musty," said one of the guys with admiration.

"I'll say!" agreed Mortimer. "Great catch for a *girl* —or for anyone," he added quickly, not wanting to offend her.

Musty felt good in all the limelight. But the incident with Ferdie had taken the joy out of it. *Why would Ferdie do that to me?* she wondered. The little girl mole was beginning to think there was something more under the ferret's skin than a burr. *Maybe he's the one who's trying to sabotage us,* she thought. *But why would he sabotage his own team?*

The next day Dusty was upset. "Now where did I put it?" he fumed. He was throwing things out of his closet left and right, making a terrible mess.

"Put what?" inquired Musty, ducking a shoe that came flying out of his door as she passed his room.

She tossed the shoe into the heap of stuff on the floor. "Wait till Mom sees this mess," she warned.

Dusty emerged from the back of his closet covered with cobwebs and dirt. "I'll clean it up," he snuffled, wiping his paw across his dirty face. *"Achoo!"* he sneezed.

"Now see what you've done!" accused his sister. "You've got your allergies all stirred up." Musty hated it when Dusty had trouble with his allergies. "What are you looking for?" she asked, a bit impatiently. "Must be important to risk getting your allergies messed up."

Dusty sneezed again. "It is," he snuffed. "I've—I've—*achoo!* I've lost my clues notebook." The private eye sneezed again and blew his nose.

"Your notebook!" exclaimed Musty. That was Dusty's most important item, where he kept all the leads and clues for each mystery he was trying to solve.

"When did you last have it?" asked the girl mole.

"At practice last night, but I'm sure I brought it home. I thought it might have dropped out of my pocket back in my closet," he explained. Sneezing again, he looked at his sister. "What will I do without it? It's my brains. I can't do a thing about this mess with the Molers unless I find it."

"Dusty Mole! What are you doing?" cried Mother Miranda, stepping into his room. "Come out of there at once! This dust is terrible for your allergies."

Sneezing and wheezing, Dusty meekly obeyed his mother.

"I'll clean up in here, Mom," offered Musty.

"You're a good girl, Musty," said Mother, taking Dusty into the kitchen for some medicine.

"Thanks, sis," said her twin. "I'll help you out sometime."

Musty began putting things back in the closet. Under a pair of sneakers Musty saw an old photograph lying on the floor. Picking it up, she froze. The picture was of a ferret family. Although it had been taken some time ago, she recognized the face of Ferdie Ferret smiling up at her.

What is this doing here? she wondered. *I wonder if Ferdie came here and took Dusty's notebook? Perhaps he dropped this accidentally.*

Musty started to run out the door to tell Dusty. Then she stopped. *What can Dusty do about it?* she wondered. *He should rest and take care of his allergies this evening. I'll see if I can't find out why this picture is here. Maybe I'll find Dusty's notebook too.*

TRIP TO SHREWSVILLE

Musty quietly left the burrow by the back way, so that her mother and Dusty wouldn't question where she was going. It was late afternoon, and the smells of summer surrounded her.

The girl mole had a bold plan. She intended to go to Ferdie's home and see what she could find out. That way Dusty could rest and get better, and she could help.

It was getting darker in the underground as she drew near the Upstairs Connection. The Connection was a long tunnel leading aboveground, where Shrewsville was located. The ferret family lived just outside Shrewsville, in shallow burrows under the ground.

The little mole was getting a bit edgy. Just ahead she could see the old lamplighter, already lighting the lights in the tunnel. She shivered, although the underground was warm tonight. It was always scary to go upstairs, and Shrewsville was where the feared Sammy Shrew lived with his son. She was glad that Sammy, Sr., was in jail.

Now she was coming to the long stretch of tunnel leading upstairs where there were no streetlights. She hurried along, humming a little tune to herself to quiet her nerves.

Suddenly a terrible thought came to her. *What if Sammy Shrew, Sr., had escaped from jail already?* Musty continued her nervous little tune as her feet fairly flew toward Shrewsville. She would feel a bit more safe in the village with the streetlights and little shops.

Coming up out of the tunnel, Musty saw a sign pointing toward Shrewsville. Breathing a sigh of relief, she quickly passed through the village. There was no sign of Sammy or his father.

Just outside the village, a sign that said "Ferret Family" pointed down a path. Musty turned off the road before she came to the path leading to the ferrets' home. She wanted to come up behind their burrow and see what she could discover.

As she made her way through the forest, she nervously glanced over her shoulder. The night sounds of the upstairs were unfamiliar, making her wish she had her brother with her.

Just ahead Musty heard voices and recognized the voice of Ferdie. He and his father were cleaning up

around their burrow, using a rake and wheelbarrow. The mole hid behind a tree, straining to hear their conversation.

Ferdie was speaking. "I did the best I could, Pop."

"Bah! You never do your best. If you did, you'd be on the first string by now. You're letting those moles get ahead of you."

"But, Pop! What can I do? Some of them pitch better than I do. Flash Mole is a great hitter. He's batting .347 this year!"

"You're just lazy!" argued his father. "How will you ever make the pro team if you don't even try?"

"But I do try, Pop! I've done all I can to make it harder for the others to practice and get ahead. I've done everything you said. I even pushed a girl on our

team down into the dirt," said the little fellow with shame in his voice. "And I broke into their burrow the other day and stole Dusty Mole's clues notebook so he couldn't remember all the stuff I did."

Musty clapped her hand over her mouth. She had already heard all she needed to hear. How she wished Dusty or someone else were along so they could confront the ferrets with their wrongdoing.

"You're too soft!" exploded his father.

"But, I'm on their *team!*" sputtered Ferdie. "What good will all this do?"

"They can't play well with all the things happening to the team, silly!" said Mr. Ferret. "Sometimes I don't think you have a brain in your head. If they don't play well, you'll play better. Then you can make the first string and win the All-Star Award. You'll never have a chance to play on a pro team if you don't get the All-Star Award. Do you understand?"

Ferdie's father glared at his son over the wheelbarrow.

Ferdie nodded numbly. Tears were coming down his cheeks. "But I don't want to play pro ball, Dad. Not if it means having everyone on my team as an enemy."

"Forget about friends!" screamed Mr. Ferret. "Think about one thing—WINNING! Do you hear me? I said

winning is the only important thing. It doesn't matter how you do it!"

Ferdie's father stormed into the burrow leaving his poor son in tears. Musty could hear his sobs as he continued raking.

Scrambling from her hiding place, Musty ran for the tunnel to the underground as fast as she could go. She was no longer angry with Ferdie for what he was doing. She only pitied him now. He was being driven by his father, who wanted him to win so badly that nothing else mattered.

Why does Mr. Ferret feel that way? she wondered. *And what can I do? How can I help Ferdie?*

THE MOLERS' STRATEGY

Musty arrived home breathless, anxious to tell her twin brother all she had heard. Dusty was feeling much better since taking his allergy medicine. After Musty told him what she had heard, his reaction was much like hers. Together they decided that something had to be done to help Ferdie Ferret.

The next day Dusty called a meeting of the Mystery Club and explained all they had discovered. All the members felt sympathy for the poor ferret who was being forced to do mean things so that he could win the All-Star Award.

"We've got to do something to help him," agreed Snarkey. "But what?"

"If he's allowed to continue, he may really hurt someone, and that would be awful," observed Otis.

"I think I have an idea, if we could get him to listen," said Snarkey.

All the club members looked at the Molers' best pitcher, who had almost recovered from his injury.

"What would you think if we helped Ferdie become an All-Star?" he asked. "Perhaps his father would back off and allow him just to enjoy playing."

"How could we do that?" asked Dusty. "He's not good enough to win the award."

"We have another week until the big game. What if we were to do nothing but practice pitching with him?" suggested Snarkey. "He does his best at that."

"If we got Coach to agree, I would work with him. I think we could develop his pitching a lot by then," continued Snarkey. "He really has potential, but he won't cooperate with any of us so he hasn't improved much. I would be free to work with him all week."

"But Snarkey! You haven't pitched for two weeks. You need to practice yourself. We need you for the big game," protested Morty.

"Don't you get it, Mort? What I'm saying is, I won't pitch the big game. I'll let Ferdie do it. I'll work with him and help him do it."

Penney gasped, "Oh, Snarkey, I think that would be wonderful! What a great sport you are to do such a thing."

"It would be fine if Coach goes for it," said Otis cautiously. "It might mean the championship. We could lose without you, Snarkey."

"Well, I for one say it's worth it," encouraged Dusty. "How many of you agree?" All the members voted to give Ferdie his chance at being an All-Star.

"The next thing is how to go about it," said Dusty. "Someone will need to talk to Ferdie and tell him we know everything. We'll have to persuade him to work with us."

"Now there I draw a blank," said Snarkey. "He won't talk to me." The others agreed that Ferdie didn't know any of them well enough to listen to them.

"I *think* he'd listen to me," said Penney quietly.

"You!" exploded Otis. "Why would he listen to *you*?"

"Yeah," gruffed Morty. "You're just a girl."

"Precisely!" said Penney. "You see, he—uh—what I mean is—"

"What Penney means is that she and Ferdie are well—special friends," interrupted Musty, helping her embarrassed friend say what she needed to say.

"Well, I never thought—" began Otis.

"I guess none of us did, Otis." Dusty laughed. "That's great, Penney. I'm sure you can get him to listen. Now the rest of us need to talk to the coach and see if he will let us do this."

With excitement the club meeting broke up with the members each scurrying to some important duty before they would approach Ferdie. The question was, *Would it work, and would Ferdie let them help him?*

The next day was an astonishing day. The club members received the go-ahead from Coach Malley to have Snarkey train Ferdie. Penney spoke to Ferdie, and he agreed to meet with the club members.

When Ferdie met with them, he explained that his father was Sammy Shrew's cousin. The ugly shrew had pushed Mr. Ferret too far, always bragging about Sammy, Jr., and telling him Ferdie was no good. This had made Mr. Ferret desperate to have Ferdie win the All-Star Award.

When the club members laid their plans before the ferret, he was so overwhelmed he almost cried. "Why would you do this for me," he asked, "after all the mean things I've done?"

"Ferdie, there's a whole lot more at stake than winning the game and the All-Star Award," reasoned Dusty. "Your future is on the line. You need help, and we all agree that's more important than winning a game."

"It's the team spirit and how we play the game that matters," agreed Morty.

"Coach Malley is really big on building up his players," added Otis. "He cares more about their future than any championship. That's why he is willing to risk it all for you."

"Now, let's make tracks to Moler Park and turn this ferret into a champion," cried Snarkey. Cheering wildly, the club members and Ferdie ran out of the clubhouse.

ALMOST OUT

The next few days the Molers worked Ferdie very hard, teaching him all the finer points of pitching. To everyone's delight, it was soon apparent that the ferret had pitching talent. This encouraged the team to work even harder with him.

One evening Ferdie came to Dusty's home and returned the notebook he had stolen. After apologizing for taking it, Ferdie told Dusty that he had told his father all that had happened and how the team was working with him.

"My dad didn't believe it when I told him," he said.

"Well, maybe he will when he sees you play in the game," replied Dusty.

"I sure hope I can be all you want, Dusty. I don't want to let the team down," said the ferret in a worried tone.

"Look, Ferdie, there is no way you can let us down. Win or lose, we've gained your friendship, and you've gotten yourself straightened out. That's all that counts," said the wise junior agent, putting a paw around his new friend.

The day of the big game arrived, and with great excitement the Molers left their locker-room. They had agreed that no matter what happened, whether winning or losing, Ferdie would pitch the last three innings.

"It's a lot of pressure for the little kid," said Otis as he and Dusty brought the balls and equipment out.

"It is, but I believe he's up to it. He's really done well the last couple of days in practice," said Dusty.

"How well he'll do in the game is still the question," insisted Otis. "But it's worth it, no matter what."

The first few innings of the game were scoreless. The teams were evenly matched. In the fourth inning, though, a ball was missed by the Molers, and a run was scored by the Shrews. From that minute on the Molers seemed to fall apart. The Shrews went ahead by three runs.

In the bottom of the sixth inning Snarkey mumbled to Flash that things didn't look too good for the Molers.

"Yeah, and Ferdie starts pitching next inning. What a lot of pressure for him." Flash groaned.

Ferdie went to the mound with butterflies in his stomach. Looking up into the stands, he saw his father and heard him yelling for him. His first two innings whizzed by with no runs scored by either team.

"The ferret kid's doing well," commented Coach Malley to Dusty, as they stood on the sidelines.

Just then the umpire called, "Ball one."

Dusty groaned, "Oh no. I hope he's not starting to fall apart. If he does, will you change pitchers, Coach?"

"No way," said Coach Malley with determination. "I said he'd pitch the last three innings, and I'll stay with that decision."

Dusty looked at him with admiration. "You're a true sport, to risk the championship this way."

"I'd rather risk the championship than Ferdie's future," answered the coach.

Suddenly the crack of the bat drew them back to the game. A fly ball to right field was caught by the Molers for an easy out. Then Dusty and the coach watched in disbelief as a ground ball rolled into their shortstop's glove. He threw to first in plenty of time, giving them two outs.

"Coach! He's got his curve ball working!" yelled Dusty, jumping up and down and thumping the coach

on the back. "Come on, Ferdie! You can do it!" he encouraged.

A hush settled over the park as Sammy Shrew, Jr., stepped up to bat. He was the Shrews' best hitter. Ferdie's heart was pounding as he pitched a fastball.

Sammy hit the ball far into left field, making the Moler left fielder run backward with his eye on the ball. Making a high lunge, he caught it just as it was about to clear the fence. The game was tied in the top of the ninth!

It was almost unbelievable! The Moler fans were going wild! Now they were up to bat with the chance for the go-ahead run. The moles held their breath as their first batter, Snarkey, hit a high fly ball deep into center field. It looked like it could be a home run, but the Shrew's center fielder snagged it for an out. Groans and gasps came from the Molers.

The disappointed fans settled back in their seats. The next batter was their ace, Flash Mole. The moles were confident he would give them the run they needed to win.

THE ALL-STAR

Another hush came over the ball park as the first sign was given and a strike was called. The Shrew pitcher, Sammy, Jr., was pitching his best to Flash. The moles watched in disappointment as the umpire called strike two. Their hearts sank into their shoes as they feared the championship was slipping away from them. *Would the game go into extra innings?*

"Only one more out!" Dusty groaned. "And now Ferdie is up to bat!" Snarkey had worked so hard on Ferdie's pitching, he had not practiced batting at all with him. Ferdie was sure to strike out.

Dusty felt sick. If Ferdie struck out now, Mr. Ferret would think his son was a failure and all their plans to help him would be for nothing. The detective mole could hardly bear to look as the ferret stepped up to bat.

"CRACK!" Ferdie hit the first ball thrown. Dusty opened his eyes in time to see a blur flying high toward the outfield fence. With his heart in his mouth, Dusty watched it clear the fence. It was a home run! Ferdie flew around the bases as if on wings!

Sammy Shrew, Jr., threw his cap on the field and jumped up and down in a rage. The Shrew coach paced the field, watching the ferret run for home and the championship.

As Ferdie crossed home plate, his happy teammates hoisted him to their shoulders screaming, "Ferdie! Ferdie! Ferdie!" The one cheering loudest was Snarkey Mole, who had made it all happen. For several minutes all was pandemonium as the Molers congratulated themselves on their victory.

Then the loudspeaker called the teams to attention for the presentation of the awards. The first one to be given was the championship trophy, and then came the All-Star Award. A beaming Ferdie received it and held his trophy proudly for the photographer. When asked for a brief comment, he gave high praise to his coach, team, and Snarkey Mole.

A surprise to everyone was a trophy for sportsmanship, being given that year for the first time. "This Outstanding Sportsmanship Award is presented to... Snarkey Mole," boomed the announcer over the microphone. "He unselfishly trained Ferdie Ferret to All-Star status, after being injured himself, and is a fine example of what this game is all about."

Snarkey walked across the field, stunned to receive such an honor, as his teammates screamed themselves hoarse. "Snarkey! Snarkey! Snarkey!" they cheered their friend.

The Shrews, wearing long faces, trooped onto the field to receive the second place trophy. Sammy Shrew, Jr., tears blurring his eyes, received the trophy for Outstanding Player of the Second Place Team.

Ferdie watched as his scrappy little cousin walked slowly back to his disappointed team. Suddenly the ferret shot across the field and put his paw around his cousin Sammy, Jr.

"Hey, fellas!" he yelled to the photographers. "How about a picture of me with my cousin Sammy? Being winners runs in this family, you know."

Sammy could hardly believe what was happening. Ferdie was sharing the honors with him. *He called me his cousin,* thought the overwhelmed little shrew. All his life Sammy had been ashamed of his family. Now the Molers were actually cheering for him. "SAMMY! SAMMY! SAMMY!" they cheered and chanted. Longtime hurts between the moles, ferrets, and shrews were mended that day.

A lone figure stood along the sidelines, watching the happy scene. It was Ferdie's father. "I'm so proud of you, son," he said, coming to Ferdie and giving him a hug. "I can't believe the way you played. You were wonderful!"

"*They* were wonderful, Dad," said Ferdie, waving a paw toward his admiring teammates. "They were the ones who taught me to pitch and gave me the chance to do it. Snarkey could have won this game easily, but he let me do it," he said with a catch in his voice.

Coach Malley stepped up with an outstretched paw. "Wonderful player, your son," he said happily to Mr. Ferret.

"Thank you, sir," replied Ferdie's father. "All the credit must go to you. I've not taught him right in this. Winning was most important to me. I can see today that he has learned more than how to play ball with you. I am deeply grateful."

"I hope you will allow him to continue on our team," said the coach. "I know you had hoped he would play pro ball."

Mr. Ferret put his paw around his son lovingly. "I think Ferdie is right where he needs to be," he said proudly. "I believe he's already with a *pro* team."

Then Mr. Ferret turned to Sammy, Jr., who was standing a little apart from the others. "Great game, Sammy. Your dad would have been proud of you."

Sammy wiped a grimy paw across his face. "Yeah, I guess he would," he agreed.

"Who are you staying with, son, now that your dad is in—uh—gone?" asked Ferdie's father.

"Aw, I'm getting along by myself," stammered Sammy in an embarrassed tone.

Speaking kindly, Mr. Ferret said, "Why don't you come and live with us till your dad can be with you again, Sammy? Maybe together we can learn more about the kind of life Coach Malley and his team have shown."

"I'd really like that," agreed Sammy. "That is, if Ferdie would like it," he added, looking at his All-Star cousin.

"Sure!" said Ferdie. "We can practice together. Who knows—someday we may be playing on the same team."

Coach Malley and Snarkey walked back to their team, leaving the ferrets and their cousin to get acquainted with each other.

"I wouldn't mind having a shrew on my team, would you, Snarkey?" asked Coach Malley, putting his paw around the mole.

"Not at all. With the Molehole Mystery Club on our side, this team can stand anything," he said, with a wink at Dusty.

Laughing and joking, the coach and Dusty and Snarkey headed for the locker-room to help the Molers celebrate their championship.

THROUGH THE SPYGLASS

Would you like to know how Sammy Shrew, Jr., is getting along living with his cousin Ferdie Ferret? Take a look through my spyglass, and you will see them living as a happy family and having lots of fun together.

Often on winter evenings they play games, and Mr. Ferret tells them stories about the fun he had when he was a young ferret. Now that Mr. Ferret is more relaxed about his ball playing, Ferdie is really enjoying himself with his team.

Ferdie's father, realizing that he had not taught his son good sportsmanship, now encourages him to make it the most important part of his athletic life.

With guidance and encouragement, Sammy Shrew, Jr., has become a much better shrew and has become well liked, not only in Shrewsville but with his mole friends as well.

The animals have learned something about life that sometimes parents and kids need to learn. Although sports are fun, they aren't everything. What is most important is that we do our best and play the game fairly, treating other teams and players with respect.

A couple of time-tested truths found in the Word of God say, "Do unto others as you would have them

do unto you," and, "Love your neighbor as yourself."
By following these principles, we can learn from the
games we play how to excel, live a happy life, and be
at peace with those around us.

Another beautiful verse from God's Word says,
"Physical training is of some value, but godliness has
value for all things, holding promise for both the
present life and the life to come" [1 Timothy 4:8;
New International Version]. In other words, not only is
it important to exercise and train our bodies, but we
also need to exercise ourselves spiritually. We can do
this by reading God's Word, memorizing it, and making it a part of our lives.

UNDERGROUND
"DIG-TIONARY"

FERRET (fer´it): An animal of the weasel family, used long ago for hunting rabbits and rats.

The ferret, an endangered species in the United States, lives in our Western prairie states. Ferrets feed on prairie dogs and nest in the prairie dogs' burrows below the ground. They are good hunters, especially of rabbits. The word *ferret* can sometimes be used as a verb meaning "to hunt."

The ferret is much larger than a mole or shrew, usually 15″ to 18″ long. It may be recognized by its yellowish-brown or buff-colored body. Ferrets have black-tipped tails and black feet. They also have a black fur mask on their faces, giving them a bandit-like appearance.

Ferrets are nocturnal animals, which means they move about mostly at night. Because of this, not much is known about this mysterious animal, one of our rarest mammals.

JOIN
MOLEHOLE MYSTERY
CLUB

Would you like to join the Molehole Mystery Club? This will entitle you to receive your very own Molehole Mystery Club ID card and Dusty's free newsletter. The newsletter will be filled with clues and mysteries you can solve and lots of fun things to do.

The newsletter will share things with you from God's Word that will help you live a happy life as a child of God. My spyglass shows me some wonderful words from the Bible that you need to remember always.

These verses are the Molehole Mystery Club Motto, and you will need to memorize them to become a member. The words are found in the Bible [1 Thessalonians 5:21 and 22]: "Test everything. Hold on to the good. Avoid [stay away from] every kind of evil" *(New International Version)*.

We'll be looking for your membership application for our club. See you in the next Molehole adventure story. Happy reading!

MOLEHOLE MYSTERY SERIES

Dusty and Musty are at it again, solving more mysteries. And you can be a part of the fun!

Join in with Dusty and the rest of the club and experience lots of neat adventures with them in **Dusty Mole, Private Eye; Secret at Mossy Root Mansion; The Gypsies' Secret; Foul Play at Moler Park; The Upstairs Connection;** and **The Hare-Brained Habit**.

All of the books in the Molehole Mystery Series are filled with the underground mystery and intrigue of your junior agent friends Dusty and

Musty Mole and the rest of the Mystery Club: Morty, Millard, Alby, Penney, Snarkey, Alfred, and Otis.

Don't let the villianous Sammy Shrew catch you by surprise. You can be on the inside track by joining the Molehole Mystery Club.

If you would like to be a member of the Molehole Mystery Club and hear more about the adventures of Dusty and Musty, fill out the card below and send it in. By being an official member, you will receive six issues of the newsletter, *The Underground Gazette,* and your own I.D. card.

MOLEHOLE MYSTERY CLUB MEMBERSHIP APPLICATION

DATE:_____

NAME: _____

ADDRESS: _____

CITY, STATE: _____ ZIP:_____

AGE: _____ BIRTHDATE: _____

___ CHECK HERE IF YOU HAVE MEMORIZED
    OUR MOTTO VERSES,

1 THESSALONIANS 5:21 - 22.
"Test everything. Hold on to the good. Stay away from every kind of evil."

Wait a minute, you mean the card is missing! Well you can still be a member of the Molehole Mystery Club by just sending in your name and address to:

Molehole Mystery Club
Lock Box 10064
Chicago, IL 60610-0064

Molehole Mystery Club
Lock Box 10064
Chicago, IL 60610-0064